T0132231

Little Book of Psalms

A Calling to the Lord
a Blessing from His Word

D. Ferro

Copyright © 2019 D. Ferro.

All rights reserved. No part of this book may be used or reproduced by any means, graphic, electronic, or mechanical, including photocopying, recording, taping or by any information storage retrieval system without the written permission of the author except in the case of brief quotations embodied in critical articles and reviews.

WestBow Press books may be ordered through booksellers or by contacting:

WestBow Press
A Division of Thomas Nelson & Zondervan
1663 Liberty Drive
Bloomington, IN 47403
www.westbowpress.com
1 (866) 928-1240

Because of the dynamic nature of the Internet, any web addresses or links contained in this book may have changed since publication and may no longer be valid. The views expressed in this work are solely those of the author and do not necessarily reflect the views of the publisher, and the publisher hereby disclaims any responsibility for them.

Any people depicted in stock imagery provided by Getty Images are models, and such images are being used for illustrative purposes only. Certain stock imagery © Getty Images.

ISBN: 978-1-9736-4811-6 (sc)
ISBN: 978-1-9736-4812-3 (e)

Library of Congress Control Number: 2018914491

Print information available on the last page.

WestBow Press rev. date: 12/13/2018

Little Book of Psalms

A Calling to the Lord
a Blessing from His Word.

Alter

Let me remember your blessing
let me decide to be glad
remember him how he watches over
my enemies are about me I rest
if I have not it is given
let my heart be his alter
when testing comes don't forget its reason
resist evil decide to be glad
showing faith
trembling weeping and grief will work your faith out lean not on
your own understanding his ways are not your ways his thought
are higher than yours blessing god continually the desert is
temporary lean on him my lord my god my father remember
when you are tested being obedient you will walk out of the desert
glowing.

Sunday Morning

We are gather together in his name.
He walks the isles touching the hungry the dead and
broken lives.
The hem of his garment is more life than all the Earth.
His eyes heal just for loves sake.
God is perfect in all his ways who is like God there is
no other. We are the Heart beat of our Father.
Rejoice is the song of the chosen.
His eyes meet are eyes.
As He walk though us Filling us with his presents.
blessed is my soul for touching the hem of his garment.
He makes my face to shine.
Amen.

Nail

Hear the Whip as it Sings. To Find Its Mark Pulling the flesh to the bone. See the Crown of thorns pushed into his Place. The blood flowing feel the rough sharp Nails. Place them into bone mingled in agony. And the lungs cry out. Heaven hides her Face. He Is Lifted Up. Father Father. Is the voice of Eternity. Salvation has come for us. Blessed are the people that find Jesus the Lord.

Amen.

Refection of One

I AM one. Father. Son. And Holy spirit. I am
three body soul and spirit. I am made in my Fathers
image. They are one because I am one. I live as three.
The Lord God is One. We worship one God. I am
three body soul and spirit. I am one.
I AM. Father Son. and Holy Spirit. And you are
made in my Image. I AM ONE.

God Uses

Storms makes you look at the Lord.

Circumstances makes you think of the Lord.

Trusting. in humans lets me believe God.

Emotions puts the heart for the Word.

Life is not easy.

We are blessed in the name of the Lord.

Amen.

Hedge

When I was rebellious. You chastised me. I was covered in mud and mire. Lord you washed me and placed me on my feet. Darkness was on me. Your word was my light and my path. Mercy called and fell into my Heart. Father you lifted me up, and put my enemies down. When I woke your eyes were on me. My heart knew it and darkness fail. I will sing to the Lord for ever. His love is my covering. His heart is mine. I will sing forever. My enemy shall see and parish.

Work

Lord bless the work of my Heart. It neither for or against me. It lives for its own. It grieves and makes happiness to Itself. And takes me along for the day. Heart you think not for eternity nor for time you only desire your own path. Lord change my heart that it may know you and love your ways. Its plant seeds of desire all to its own and sleeps not. Before I wake It pleads for itself. Lord give your Heart and take mine away. That I may find rest for my soul.

Bless You Father for your HEART.

33

I AM so afraid. Fear has taken hold. There coming, cover in sweat. Now Its Red in great drops. Oh take this away from me. I want to run. My body trembled in fear. They will kill me. Great pain my Heart knows it. Please get me out of this. All have left me my body in Greif. I have given myself over to the enemy. My agony is so great flesh torn my blood everywhere. They beat me. My limbs shaking uncontrollable My tongue sticking in my mouth thirst unbearable. My hands and feet are in agony each breath my last. All have forsaken me. My Father My Father were are you. My beard torn from my face. They hit and break my teeth. .My body shakes in such great pain. I have done them no wrong. They mock me for doing right. My Father I hurt, I AM close to death .they price my side, Now my hour is come, To do my Fathers will because my Father loves you and I love my Father. I give my life. Know what I have done for you, that you may be in his present. And his heart may rejoice. THIS IS MY LOVE. And he lowered his head and took away our sins from a blood soak cross. Finished

Secret Place

Prayer you woke me with kindness. Faithfulness
with tears. Compassion to my Lord. Who like is you.
My God you are so much for me to understand. Soul
you rejoice you now your visitation. How can I share
his way it is unspeakable. Father give me your Heart
you wake me. My soul is blessed in the
SECRET PLACE.

Vail

She moves through the people. Dressed in shame and guilt. It matters not that I may touch him. She anoints his head with oil. They see and know me. I am guilty, but will not by turn away. I must have my Lord. Oh how she dresses his feet with her tears. With a broken heart she dries them with her her Hair. Weeping. Hold me. Broken. I will not be turned away. His Love ever present reaches her. And she is excepted.

SHE IS THE CHURCH.

Not worthy but loved. The Lord gave his life for HER. Blessed is our Father who dresses her in white. NEVER to be TURNED from his LOVE. The VAIL lifted they are ONE.

Child Eyes

For God to lift up his face to shine his Constance
Is to hold his child up in his arms. The fierceness of
his love in beauty toward his little ones. Ever mindful
his love commanded to us. He would give himself
fully. So we would know the value of his heart, Love.
Mercy. Truth. Using all the opposite things to mold us
with fire. That through the trails of life we would be
forged into his likeness. A seed is surrounded by
darkness and dies to itself. Its desire is to push to the
Light that it bears fruit. So are we designed to be in
His likeness and Image.

Voice

I have never seen your FACE Heard your Voice. Your HAND is not seen only felt. EYES I have never looked into .yet they watch me always. LOVE that I cant see protects me. SPIRIT that gives life is like the wind My son you are in the womb of the earth. Can the unborn see the Father. While he rest under the heart of the mother in the womb. But when he is born he knows his FATHER and will not go to another.

Amen.

Little One

I see Adam as a child with his hand in his Fathers hand on a walk. As he cleaves to his Fathers side and the eyes look without saying a Word. Abba and son. The Father watching with great joy as his little one sleeps. You are my beloved I will give all for you. And the little one wake seeking only his FATHER. Holding his son turning about with great laughter son to his chest. The heart of GOD speaking I AM giving all for my children. The Lord walking in the cool evening holding Adams little hand. Blessed are the children of the GOD. They have the Lords HEART.

Morning

LORD you visit me and straighten my heart. Walk with me. Take my hand. My eyes look at your word. My mouth is satisfied my soul rejoiced And my path is sure. Delight my spirit with your present. I have confessed you and you have confessed me. Your hedge is sure. Lite your wings on me that my HEART may sing in your name.

Amen.

Life

We gather all and are at loss.
We call are own and lack.
We reach to the flesh and desire its way.
God only is value and gain. His face holds love only.
There is only his word for you.
He waits as a father for a child.
You know not but his hands are ever ready for you.
Receive his Word and lack nothing.
Amen.

The Gift

Driven down to the knee.
Hands made to pray.
Heart unlocked with pain.
The weight of sorrow.
How blessed am I
The gift of suffering.
That pushes me before God.
Has molded me into happiness.
Thankful suffering has brought
life. THE GIFT.

Today

Storm is still.

Darkness is gone.

Peace and joy are at my side.

Calm is the Heart beat.

Love is my covering. Blessing run after me.

Rest is mine. Know one take me out of his hands.

His word is my path. Father your love is my light.

My heart sings and can not be silence, This the end of
those who find JESUS THE LORD.

Amen.

I am

King of Peace

Thank you Lord you have made the grains.
That have become reflection.
The days of paint into years of purpose.
The picture shows God is innocent.
Father we are lost. You are the one that takes all.
Not willing that one should parish.
Bless the Lord.

Church

Break over the walls. Let down vine Carry the bread
and water of God.
To the blind. To the lost those who are bound by dark.
They will eat and see. Drink and never thirst after
another. Bring them into the church to be filled with
the WORD.

All

In the womb we rest under are mothers heart.
Having no need for mouth, hands, feet, eyes, ears.
They are for the next life at birth.
The same in the earth. Joy, sorrow, grief,
righteousness, love, pain, loss, and truth. We are
fashion In his likeness. Salvation in Gods love. In
the womb of the earth under the Lords heart. Tested
by Fire of his word. The Father wait for his children.
Delivered into his hands.
Amen.

Thanks

Blessed is the Father and the Son and Holy Spirit.
For they are one. Thanks that we are not consumed
for are transgressions.
Blessed for your word, safety, and provisions.
Blessed is the lord God Almighty.
In Jesus name we pray. Bless his name Amen.

Dark Water

Only a few steps in so dark. Water so deep wants gone
in there is no recovery. Those on the shore saying be
quiet. If I do not cry out. My Soul move my flesh
out of the way. That the light of the rescue will not
pass me by. I cried out even more. Be quiet said
those on shore. But the captain on the boat heard me.
And pulled me in out of the dark water.
The captain said if you would have stop calling me.
You would be Lost. I was so grateful that I kissed his
feet. That's when I saw the NAIL marks. My soul that
day was saved, because the Lord my Father heard me.
In The Dark Water.

A love that lives in His word to light a path in His name.

Printed in the United States
By Bookmasters